EX
LIBRIS

The Faultlines is an ancient name given to those places where the veil between this world and the Other is thinnest. It is the place where faeries dwell, creatures creep, and magic oozes through the cracks. Recently the Faultlines have been stirring, opening up to all who wish to see, and to all who dare to venture...

For my dad

FAERIES
OF THE
FAULTLINES

AS OBSERVED & DOCUMENTED
BY IRIS COMPIET

FAERIES

As someone who has attempted to paint faeries and otherworldly beings for fifty years, I know how difficult it is to be true to the subject matter. Iris Compiet's work is an astonishing and masterful revelation of the Faery Realms. She is an artist who, with stunning alacrity, reveals the fleeting personalities of the normally unseen. Her nuanced lines vibrate with spiritual energy, chasing and ultimately expressing the illusive nature of these liminal beings.

Her work is infused with limpid washes of colour that are seemingly taken from a paintbox of hues gathered from the aurora borealis – eloquent in describing the ever-changing qualities of faery. Here are beings as witty and merry as an Irish Clurichaun as well as those of rare beauty that touch the heart and lift the soul.

Brian Froud
November 2017

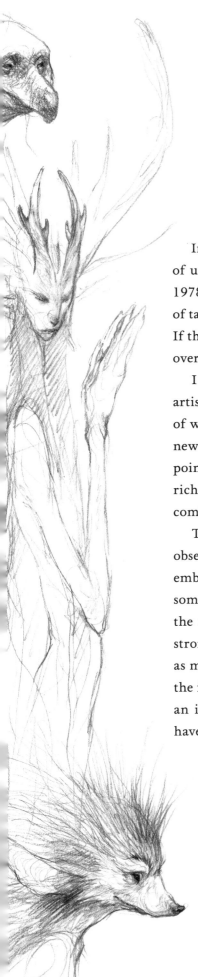

FAULTLINES

Iris Compiet has said that she was led towards her path as an illustrator of unseen worlds by the *Faeries* book that Brian Froud and I published in 1978. This is a tremendous compliment, but I think that, with her wealth of talent, she would have found her own way through those enticing woods. If there is an influence, it goes both ways; I can happily spend hours poring over the details of the creatures she invents.

I think both Brian and I were conscious of the earlier illustrators and artists in this field and their ways of imagining and representing faeries, of wanting to be part of that tradition and, at the same time, to create some new variations on those age-old themes. Iris has taken a similar starting point but has opened up many more new and distinctive pathways in this rich forest of tradition, dreams, and untold stories to provoke a wonderful combination of recognition and surprise.

These sketches have the vivid quality of field notes, things quickly observed and put down on paper before the memory fades, but they also embody the intangible qualities of the beings represented. They capture something of their elusive, flowing, and transformational nature through the mediums used and Iris's particular skills – a way of identifying so strongly with her materials that the flowing lines and washes are animated as much by nature as they are by intention. She summons and draws upon the forces that are necessary in giving life to such creatures – imagination, an intelligent curiosity, and a relentless energy. The faeries are lucky to have her!

Alan Lee
September 2020

THE FAULTLINES ARE OPEN

Within the pages of this book, you will find paintings, sketches, and short stories that I, Iris Compiet, collected on my travels through a place I've come to know as the Faultlines. The Faultlines isn't a place in the traditional sense of the word; at least, it's not just one place, but many. It's perhaps best described as areas where the veil between our human world and the world of the faeries is thinnest and we can enter a world that is still ours but slightly different. Faeries are alive right here among us but hidden behind a thin veil of Other.* Once you step beyond that veil, you will enter the Faultlines.

You may have glimpsed the veil before in a single dewdrop, in a rainbow, or even in the corner of your eye when you had the distinct feeling someone – or something – was watching you. The veil is here, always and everywhere: it is around you, beneath you, above you, behind you, and even inside you. Faeries are everywhere if you just know how to look for them.

After carefully waiting, listening, and observing, I was lucky enough to regain my Sight** into the Other. I've been granted access to the world of the faeries and gradually earned their trust, which allowed me to write, illustrate, and pass these stories on to you. It's my hope that the words on these pages, combined with the images of the faeries, will excite the senses of those seeking the Other and help them regain their Sight. Although this Sight into the world of faeries is innate to all beings and humans are born with it as children, it's often lost as we enter adulthood.

---

* Other *is another name for the world of faeries. While this world intersects with ours and is interwoven with it, most humans are no longer in touch with the Other and thus cannot access it.*
** Sight *isn't the same as vision or seeing something with your eyes. When I refer to Sight, it relates to all senses we use. The Sight into the Other requires us to use all our senses, rather than just our vision. Sometimes it is a particular smell, a light touch, a tingling sensation on the back of your neck, or a whisper on a breeze. Developing all your senses so that you are more in tune with the Other is mastering Sight.*

The images and text compiled in this book are but a small part of what I've collected during my travels. The faeries were so willing to share that I've had to make some difficult decisions about what to include. I've tried to show you as much as I can of the diversity in the Faultlines, which are inhabited not only by faeries but by many more creatures, such as gnomes, dragons, and even witches. Having met members of the Seelie and the Unseelie Court* – the so-called good and evil faeries – I would like to note that no faery is either purely good or evil: they are simply All, a state of being best described as all-encompassing. Because their notions of good and evil are so very different from ours, these pure spirits are beautiful and dangerous. Since faeries eschew categorization in human terms, geography, or theme, proceed with an open mind. Allow yourself to wander to and fro. Flitting from one faery to the other, allow yourself complete immersion. Allow yourself to See ...

Finally, a word of warning: the faeries of the Faultlines do not often trouble themselves with clothing. As they are not familiar with concepts such as "shame" or "modesty," there will be some nudity in this book, and I leave it to the viewer to read this tome at their own discretion.

And now I would like to invite you to the Faultlines: be careful where you tread, mind your head, and enjoy your stay.

Iris Compiet

---

* *The terms* Seelie *and* Unseelie *are a way to classify faery kind into two categories. Seelie, derived from the Scottish word "seilie," means happy and Unseelie, from "unseely," means unhappy. The members of the Seelie Court are faeries who are considered kinder to humans, and those of the Unseelie Court are more malicious in their ways. However, I have found that neither Court can be classified as wholly good or evil.*

of the

GREENMAN

I've come to learn that greenmen are well-known inhabitants of the Faultlines and can be found everywhere you look. These magnificent, mysterious creatures usually roam the vast forests but can also be seen strolling across the rolling hills or slumbering in sleepy meadows. In mere hours, they can cover great distances, using their knowledge of the lands to quickly make their way from place to place.

A greenman's primary task is to take care of everything that grows: they nurture young saplings, tend to new growths, gather seeds, and take care of all the foliage on the ground for the Faery of the Leaves Fallen. I have been told that it's a greenman's responsibility to ensure that the cycle of life will never break and that this is a responsibility they don't take lightly.

These benevolent creatures are wonderful storytellers, and I've been lucky enough to spend many hours in their company listening to their tales. They can talk in great detail about the smell of the grass in the early morning light and are able to weave dreams out of words alone, taking their listeners on a journey through the Faultlines like no other faery can. Their voices, akin to the sound of rustling leaves, will mesmerize the weary. Those in need of a moment's rest and quiet contemplation would do well to ask a greenman for a story.

Even though they are generally good-natured, the more advanced in age a greenman gets, the more he starts to resemble the old trees he tends to. I would advise you to beware these gnarly greenmen as they do not look kindly upon those who deliberately snap twigs or tread on raised tree roots or green saplings.

A greenman is very well
adapted to living in the forests
he tends. As he ages, he slowly
becomes part of the living and
breathing world around him.
Moss gradually attaches itself
to him and fungi start to cover
his body; it becomes more and
more difficult to distinguish
him from his surroundings.

Some greenmen have multiple eyes.
I believe this third eye, or sometimes
even extra pairs of eyes, may help
them with their task of keeping
watch. A greenman is always vigilant,
always watching; indeed, one eye
remains open at all times.

Greenmen are also
known to speak the
elusive languages
of leaves.

Many greenmen are
fluent in the various
dialects of the roots
and sing the songs
of the earth, while
others speak in the
tongue of the babbling
brooks.

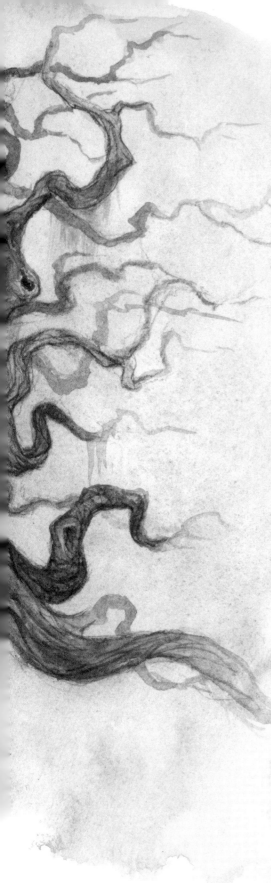

His real name long forgotten, he is now simply known as Tree. Tree is one of the three ancient Wanderers, a group responsible for carrying seedlings across the outskirts of the Faultlines. Long before the greenmen started tending the trees, it was the Wanderers who helped expand the ever-growing forests. The oldest trees in the woods, called the First, were his friends, and it was they who told him the tales of the Faultlines. He would listen to these stories and learn from them until he knew all of them by heart. In return, he would share the stories he had heard on his many travels, waxing poetic about the Valley of the Witches, the trolls of the mountains, and the Weavers of Woe.

As Tree grew older, he started to forget. At first, only the little things escaped him. Much later, Tree also forgot the names of the other Wanderers, their faces slowly fading from his memory. No longer remembering even his own name, Tree was truly alone. Finally, he could no longer remember how to wander, and that is when Tree took root. All he remembers now are the stories the First once told him. If you happen to stumble upon Tree in the meadow where he took root, I implore you to spend some time with this solitary, lonely creature and ask him to tell you one of his many stories.

Just like the greenmen, there
are other faeries that are part
of the forest and act as its protectors.

A tree faery inhabits
and protects a single
tree for its entire
lifespan.

The Faery of the Leaves Fallen, also known as the Keeper of Leaves, watches over the fallen foliage during the long months of winter. With a single touch of her fingertip, she colours the leaves from green to brown; with a single sigh, she softly blows the leaves from their branches and watches them gently drift to the ground. Where they lie, a protective blanket is formed upon the earth until spring is ready to breathe new life into the soil.

And then there are these funny little
faeries from whose heads and beards
mistletoe sprouts. Mischievous by nature,
like all faeries, they love to plant kisses
on the cheeks of travellers, granting them
safe passage, good fortune, and protection
against evil spirits.

Common woods faeries, or forest pizkies, give berries
their marvellous deep-red colour when they are
ripe for picking. These pizkies like playing tricks and
sometimes colour berries that aren't ripe or even
fit for consumption, causing severe stomach aches to
whoever is unfortunate enough to eat them.

While wisdom is innate to all faeries, the Elder Mother is one of the wisest creatures of all. She wards off evil, provides comfort, keeps all creatures in her purview safe, and offers wise counsel in times of need. I would advise you to pay your respects to the Elder Mother every time you see an elder tree, for she is always listening.

The blood of this beautiful viridescent creature has hallucinogenic properties. Luckily no faeries are killed to produce absinthe these days, but in the past she and others of her kind were hounded by poachers and killed for the precious liquid running through their veins. Now, she is one of the few remaining.

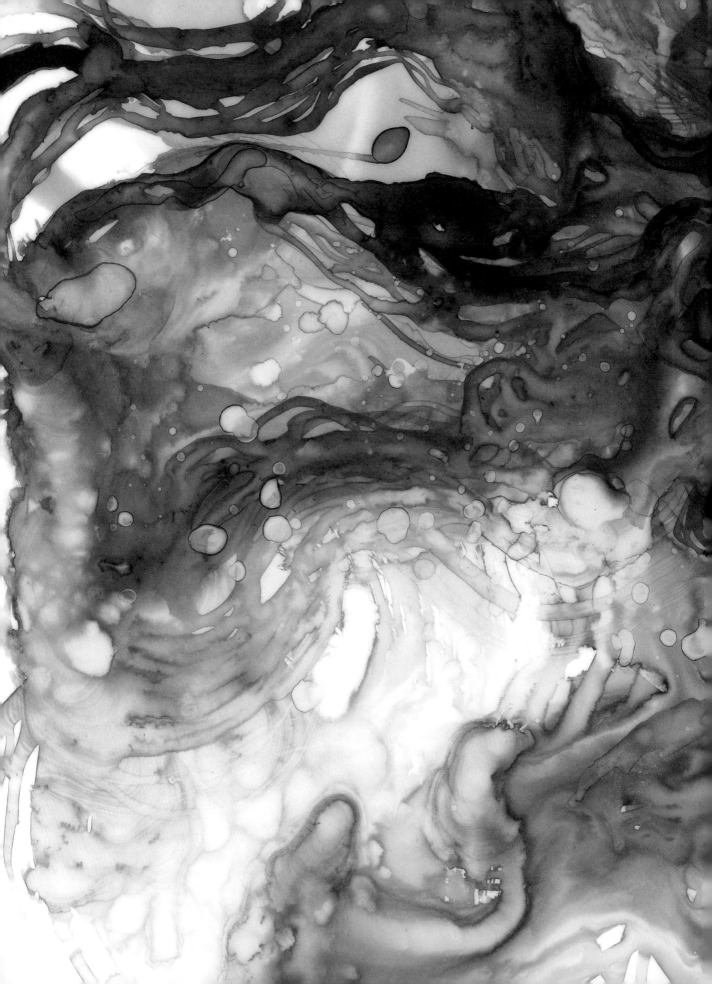

The Wyld is one of the First.
While he has seen much, he rarely
interacts with the world around
him these days. He has grown so old
that no other beings except some of the
oldest greenmen speak his language.
His gnarly limbs are warm to the touch
and resonate to his heartbeat. If you
are lucky enough to meet him, his low,
rumbling voice will leave you with an utter
sense of peace for days to come.

The Daughters of the Wyld,
whose image has rarely been
captured, are elusive creatures
akin to dryads. These maidens
only leave their chosen trees on
the first day of summer to dance
in the glowing moonlight. Catching
a glimpse of the Daughters is a sign
of great fortune. Those finding
themselves in their presence
are often overcome by feelings
of intense bliss and happiness.

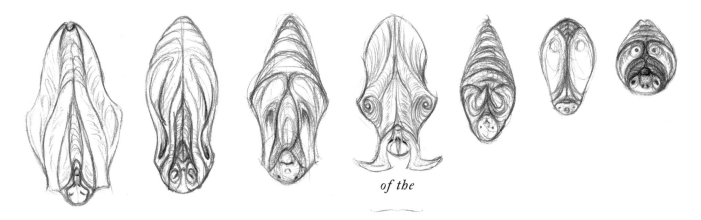

of the

FAERY CHRYSALIS

On my travels through some of the most remote parts of the Faultlines, I came across some peculiar-looking cocoons. At first, they rather resembled the chrysalides of moths or butterflies. Upon closer inspection, I noticed facial features on these polychromatic pupae, and on some of these specimens I even detected a vague outline of something best described as wings. I had never seen anything like it but assume some species of faeries go through a stage of transformation much like the Lepidoptera of our world. I made it my priority to document and observe these chrysalides without disturbing the faeries inside.

In my search for more information about these wonderful little pods, some no bigger than my thumb, I discovered stories dating back to the early Pharaohs of Egypt, who loved the cocoons for their lustrous properties and wore jewelry decorated with them.

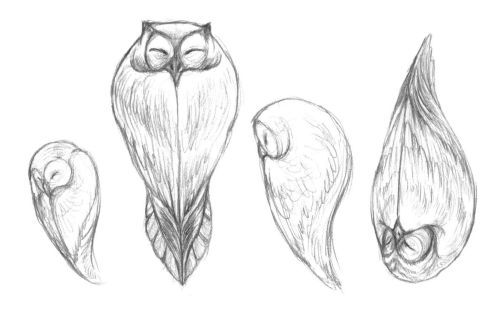

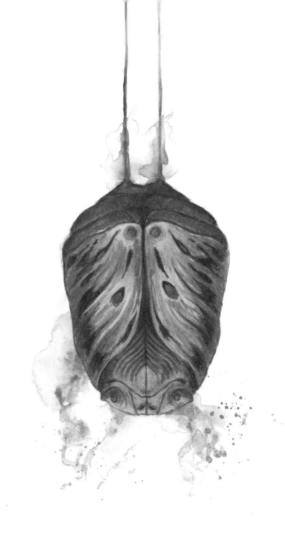

Resembling semi-precious stones and glittering like gold in the sunlight, these pupae used to be a favourite among jewellers who crafted regalia worn by kings and queens across the world. For example, jewelry decorated with these beautiful chrysalides were the height of fashion at the court of Louis XIV. Although these multicoloured pupae were sadly on the brink of extinction, the species gained a new lease on life when Marie Antoinette began favouring diamonds instead.

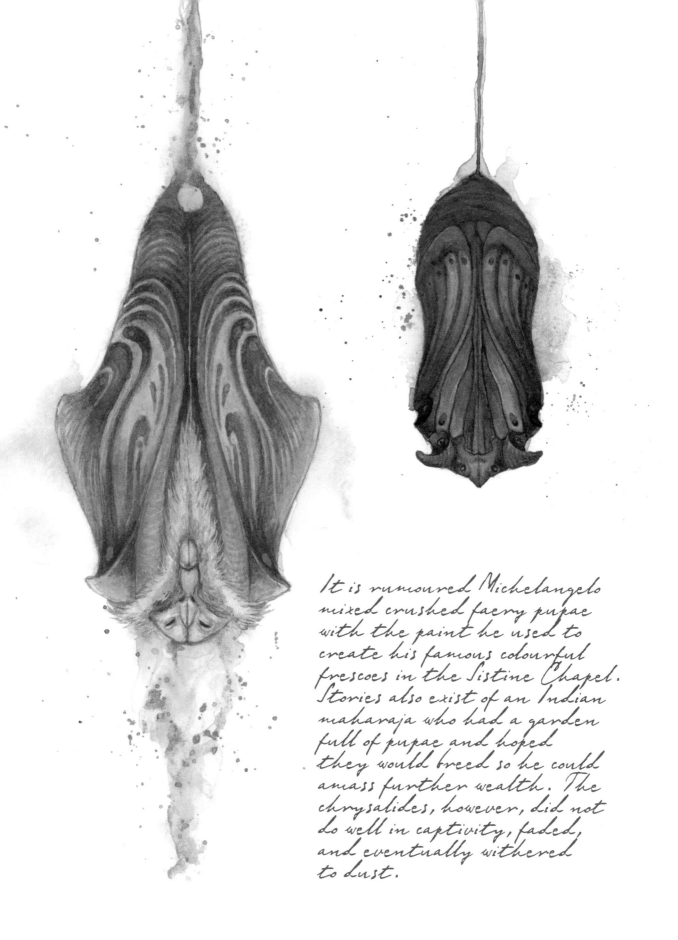

It is rumoured Michelangelo mixed crushed faery pupae with the paint he used to create his famous colourful frescoes in the Sistine Chapel. Stories also exist of an Indian maharaja who had a garden full of pupae and hoped they would breed so he could amass further wealth. The chrysalides, however, did not do well in captivity, faded, and eventually withered to dust.

The American gold rush drove this species of faery even closer to extinction as their glistening pupae were often mistaken for lumps of gold. Because they are now very rare, I implore you to leave the pupae be and never disturb them should you be lucky enough to find one.

Once, I spotted a
few peculiar faeries
with insect-like
properties.

Some of the creatures I saw had compound
eyes while others had skin covered in tiny
scales like the wings of a butterfly. These
scales are responsible for their chromatic
changes and aid in their protection and
insulation. Although their butterfly-
like tongue suggests they feed on nectar,
I've witnessed some of them using their
viscoelastic tongue to feast on other faeries.

After observing
several different
faeries of this
species I came to the
conclusion that some
of them seem to have
an exoskeleton, much
like that of common
insects. This hard
outer shell is impossible
for predators to penetrate.
Things such as spines, horns,
stingers, or their natural
chemical secretions are
just some of the ways these
creatures defend against or
kill their predators.

The various colourations of and elaborate
patterning on these creatures' exoskeletons
seems to be used as a way to communicate
with members of their own species.
Sometimes the colourations send
out a warning to any potential
predators whilst others simply
provide camouflage. All this makes
this species one of the most elusive
I have encountered in the Faultlines.
Much is yet to be discovered.

Sakura faeries are closely related to the sylphs (page 86). They are the faeries of the sakura tree, their lives tied in with the bloom: beautiful like the blossom, but very short-lived. These faeries remind us of how fleeting life and beauty really are. They perform a dance on the first day of spring, they herald new beginnings, and they sing songs of bitter endings. Their singing can be heard on the first spring breeze when the biting cold of winter is chased away. All those who take a moment to listen will feel warmth spread through their hearts as a welcoming of spring and the hope it holds.

Faeries are known for adapting to
their surroundings. Some are highly
skilled at mimicry, like these blume
faeries. Most are relatively harmless
but there are certain faeries which
will intoxicate the mind of those who
smell them. This can leave a person
in a state of euphoria and incapable of
a rational thought for several days.
The intoxicating smell will linger
around the victim and once recovered
the person will be left with a strong
feeling of befuddlement.

The prickles covering
the body of the distel
faery protect them from
being eaten by predators.
As a distel grows older their
spininess increases. Older
distels are less agile and are
easier prey. As a defence,
they develop more rigid
prickles to ward off danger.
In medieval times people
believed that a distel
faery held the cure against
baldness. Distels were collected
and sold as a miracle cure,
rendering them almost extinct.

48

Insect faeries and blume
faeries live in a symbiotic
relationship where both
species benefit from their
mutual harmony.

The blume faeries are such
masters of mimicry that
it is almost impossible to
discern them from real
flowers. Therefore, it is
important to ask the
flower if it is in fact
a flower before picking it!
One could be in for a nasty
surprise if it turns out to
be a blume faery.

The Odonata is a carnivorous faery
which can be found near bodies of
water, preferably marshes. They
feed primarily on the flesh of
smaller faeries, but when they
hunt together they are known
to best larger prey. They lure
their victims with seductive
pulsing movements of their
lower bodies, their flowing
hair snaring their prey
into a trap from which
there is no escape.
They possess double
rows of razor-sharp
teeth and even
though they do
not pose a threat
to humans, their
bite will cause an
unsightly rash
that can last
for weeks.

The body of a glimmer faery is riddled with tiny specks of gold. Their wings are delicate and fragile like those of a butterfly. If you touch these shimmering creatures, you'll find yourself covered with a gold powder also known as faery dust. As yet, a complete understanding is out of my grasp, but I do know that its unique qualities vary from faery to faery. Some dust alters your state of mind for many days, sometimes weeks.

Shroomfae are a certain kind
of faery whose skin is covered in
different types of mould, lichen,
or mushrooms, adding a beautiful
array of colour and spectacular
texture to the faery's exterior.
This outer shell also acts as a
warning to predators and can
be the perfect camouflage.

By releasing spores into
the air, these faeries
can communicate with
each other and attract
potential mates.

Even the slightest threat
will prompt a shroomfaery
to release lethal toxins into the
air. However, there are species
whose spores aren't lethal, rather,
hallucinogenic. These spores will render
any assailant confused for days and allow
the faery to escape. This is the reason
why you should take great care when you
step inside a faery ring.

Some faeries even look like mushrooms themselves. Like this Amanita faery, with its cap as vibrantly red as the cap of the highly poisonous mushroom. However, in this case the faery is completely harmless and mimics these toxic mushrooms as a defence mechanism. These little faeries lead a simple life, finding happiness in the smallest of things and taking time to appreciate what is happening around them.

Shroomfae love to get
together, forming a
perfect circle on the forest
floor. A circle of shroomfaeries
is often referred to as a faery
ring. According to several tales,
these rings are supposed to be
quite dangerous. An unlucky
human who steps into one of these
rings will be forced to dance with
the faeries, unable to stop, and
eventually going mad or even
dying from exhaustion. I have
not found conclusive evidence
to prove or disprove these
tales. There are certainly
circles which are better left
untouched and my advice
would be to never take the risk
of stepping into the wrong ring.
It's better to sit and listen outside one
of these circles. Chances are you will hear
some of the wonderful tall tales shroomfae
are known to tell.

of the

FAUN

These horned faeries, commonly known as faun, live in the wild and lonely parts of the Faultlines. When I first encountered this reclusive species, I noticed that they seemed to be very shy and cautious. However, as I spent more time with them, I came to know these creatures as gentle, kind, and willing to help those lost travellers in the outermost-reaches of the vast woodlands. They are excellent guides and these mostly solitary beings, having spent much of their life roaming the wild and remote places, can tell stories about almost everything you may encounter in the Faultlines.

For all their kindness, these charming faeries also have a knack for mischief. They are delighted when they find themselves having an audience willing to listen to their tall tales. And, once they start recounting their stories, all sense of time and place may easily get lost on them. The audience will find themselves spellbound, listening for hours and sometimes days on end, the faun taking their time to tell their story in minute detail – a dangerous thing as humans need nourishment and sleep.

When they are bored, fauns often lead travellers astray and relish the puzzled looks on their faces as they realize they are going deeper and deeper into the woods. With age, fauns become more inclined to seek solitude, finding contentment in spending their days roaming the vast woods of the Faultlines.

The horn-like protrusions
sprouting from the skulls of
fauns can look like deer antlers
but may also resemble wood.
Unlike deer, however, a faun's
horns are never shed, but instead
continue growing their entire lives.

58

Fauns are very diverse in
appearance, however, both the
males and females of this
magnificent species can be
seen roaming the Faultlines
sporting impressive horns.

The age of a faun can be determined by the size of their horns. The older a faun is, the larger their horns. Sometimes, a faun will even grow a second set as it ages. Both sets then twist and turn into elaborate curls resembling the branches of a tree.

Some fauns even adorn these elaborate curls with lichen or soft, vivid moss to further enhance their already awe-inspiring beauty. This is an important aspect of the faun's mating ritual.

I'm sad to say that even in the Faultlines, the unicorn is becoming a rare sight. These majestic, magical creatures never had to worry about natural enemies until recently.

Indeed, trolls discovered
that unicorn meat is
the sweetest, their hide
the warmest, and that
their horn is not only
worth a fortune, but
also a weapon capable of
piercing anything.

In recent years I've discovered that the unicorns are rapidly evolving. Under the threat of extinction the species seems to have adapted to a life of survival in the forests of the Faultlines. With a heightened sense of smell and hearing they are even more elusive than ever before. Their horns are no longer delicate but instead twisted and turned into a powerful defensive and offensive weapon. A unicorn can sometimes now be seen as the hunter and not the hunted.

The wetlands of the Faultlines
are treacherous and not suitable
for idle wandering. These are
the hunting grounds of the
kelpie, another solitary faery
in the guise of a horse that will
drag its victims to the bottom of
the Faultlines' murky waters.
It can remain underwater, biding
its time until an unsuspecting
human or faery strays too close
to the water's edge.

MANDRAKE

The mandrake root, or *mandragora*, is a faery known for its variety of magical uses. While famous for its hallucinogenic properties, the blood in its veins is also highly toxic. Diluted, it will induce a trance that can last for days, and the state of pure and utter happiness this liquid produces is the ultimate goal for those trying to obtain a mandrake faery. Many believe these moments of bliss far outweigh the risks involved in capturing one of these creatures.

This root faery lives deep underground, where it is safe and warm for its entire life, getting its nourishment from whatever the soil provides. According to popular myths and legends, the mandragora will start to scream and cry in a high-pitched tone when it is dug up or pulled out of the earth. This piercing sound is supposedly fatal to all who hear it.* However, this is not entirely true. The mandrake is completely harmless during certain times of the year, and under certain circumstances it is wholly safe to uproot. This knowledge has been one of the best-kept secrets in the Faultlines, known only to a select few. However, to save these wonderful beings from needless suffering this secret is shared in an attempt to prevent the decimation of the species by misinformed humans.

There are several ways to dig up a mandragora without risking premature death. Because the mandragora loves to hear stories and listen to sweet songs, the trick is to gently stroke its leaves and to talk to it in a soft and steady voice. Doing so will calm the faery, and while its wailing won't cause death, it will still cause nausea, dizziness, and bleeding from the ears on occasion.

---

*   *The screams of a mandrake are so very high in frequency that it is practically impossible for humans to hear. We can sense it as a dull pressure to our eardrums that slowly builds up until it causes bleeding from the ears, eventual rupture of the eardrums, and finally, damage to the brain.*

If prepared correctly,
the mandrake faery's
flowers and berries are quite
scrumptious. However, it is
important to note these
can't be taken by force but
instead have to be given
by the mandrake faery
freely if one wants to
prevent a bitter taste.

Indulging in too many
of these delicacies,
however, will cause
serious stomach aches.

The mandrake looks like an extremely chubby, and sometimes ugly, baby.

There are several species of mandragora, all of which have different colour variations and body shapes. Often mistaken for vegetables such as the common carrot or beetroot, they might pose a threat to those who unwittingly uproot one.

Mandragoras are believed
to bring good fortune. Some
people have even tried to
cultivate them and keep
them in flowerpots. As
these little faeries don't
flourish in captivity, no
amount of storytelling
or singing will pacify
them under these
circumstances.

There are tales of human
babies being stolen from their
cribs, beds, or prams and
exchanged for a faery.
The babies snatched from
the comfort of their home
are taken by faeries like the
skypta. The faeries left
behind in the human world
are often called changelings.
At first, these faeries very
much look like healthy,
ordinary babies, but as they grow
older they start to transform into old,
deformed, sickly, and sometimes even hostile
creatures that no longer resemble either
human or faery.

The skypta is one species of faery known for stealing human babies. A skypta will latch on to them from the very first breath they take. She will lie in wait for the perfect moment to snatch a child from its crib, leaving her own deformed offspring behind. The love she feels for these pure, pink babies is completely overwhelming and unlike anything we know. Unable to cope with this love, the human baby turns into a creature that is no longer recognizable as human. No longer of interest to the skypta, she will leave it in a crib in exchange for another child.

I was sitting on top of a mountain overlooking the vast Faultlines when my eye was drawn to a formation of rocks half-buried beneath the earth, moss, and grass. I had already wondered why I hadn't seen any giants stomping across the plains as they did in the various tales I had heard about these big, lumbering creatures.

Apparently, all the giants of the Faultlines are asleep. Waiting for what, no waking creature here seems to know. Their bodies have been overgrown with plant life, which has slowly turned them into the hills and mountains that make up the diverse landscapes of this wondrous place. As I've explored the Faultlines I've come across various suspected giants, such as this particular rock formation, which had a barely visible face and a slightly opened eye; it would therefore seem the giants are slowly waking up. More exploration is warranted to learn about these magnificent creatures.

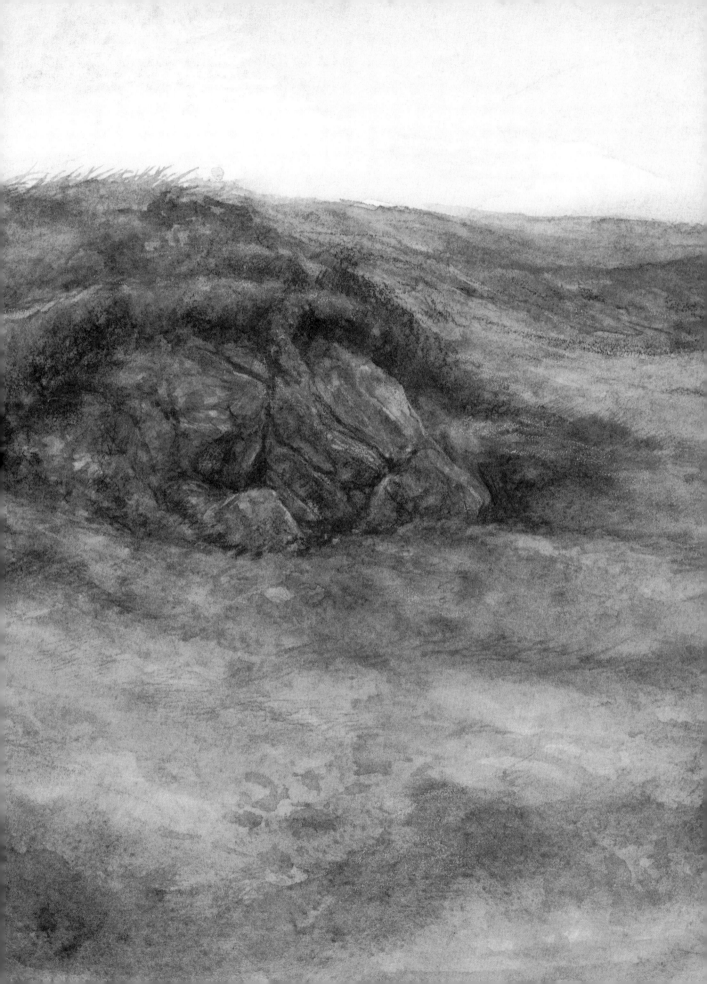

The bogs and swamps of the Faultlines
are home to wisps, who often dance in the
night sky under the light of a silver moon.
From a distance, they look like tiny, ghostly,
blueish lights and are often mistaken for fireflies.
Unlike fireflies, however, these faeries are tricksters
who enjoy leading travellers astray with their
entrancing songs and dances.

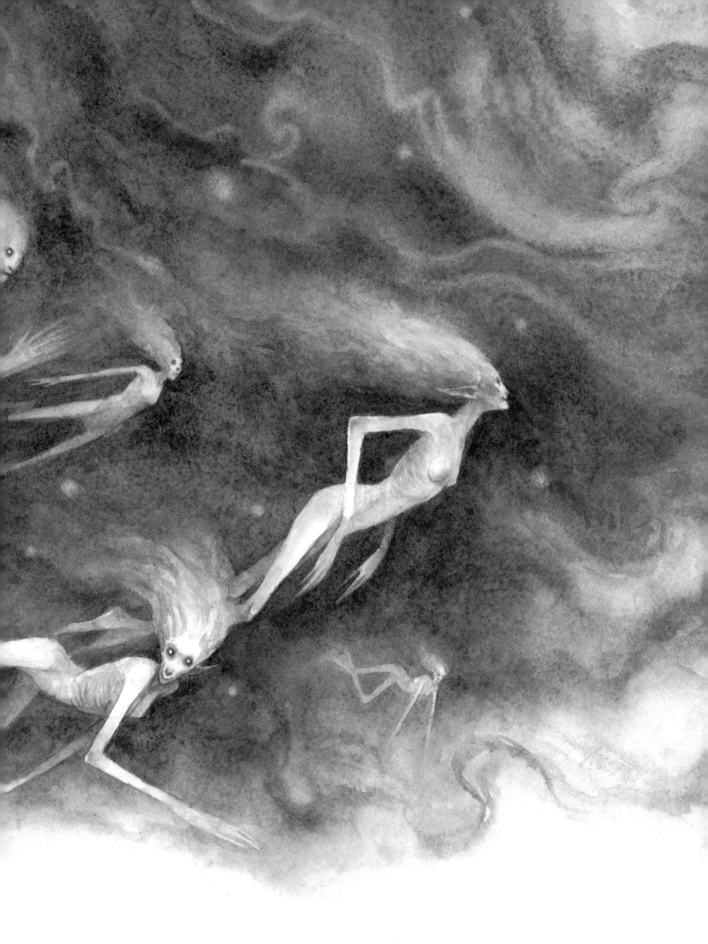

My first encounter with the faeries called silfs, or sylphs, was at the Godafoss waterfall in Iceland. As the day was drawing to a close, I could see them dancing amidst the spray of the waterfall in the last rays of sunlight. Their lives are as fleeting and delicate as the iridescent rainbows they create. Their dances are a sight of beauty and often thought to be a sign of hope and good fortune to come.

The songs of harpy faeries are so mesmerizing that sailors are powerless to ignore their sweet melodies, causing many ships to crash on the Faultlines' jagged rocks. The harpy's song is every bit as dangerous as that of the siren.

It is said that some of their songs have healing powers and that only those deemed worthy have ever been fortunate enough to hear them. (More on harpy faeries on page 103).

Finding a faery feather is very
rare indeed, as these creatures
do not often lose one of their
precious, colourful feathers.
Finding one is considered a sign
of good fortune, but it is even
more so when it is given freely.
These feathers are imbued
with powerful magic, and some
kinds of feathers are more
powerful than others. Anyone
in possession of this precious
artifact will be successful in
their endeavours. Rumour has
it Shakespeare wrote his famous
plays using a quill made from
one of these feathers.

of the

TREE OF ALL

When you find your way to the centre of the Faultlines, you will set your eyes upon a truly magical sight, for this is the beating, living heart of the Faultlines. Surrounded by the living standing stones that guard this ancient sentinel, you will find yourself in the presence of the Tree of All. This primordial tree is the gateway to all that is Other: it is both male and female, and life begins in its roots and leaves. A beacon of hope that calls out to those pure of heart and soul, human and faery alike are drawn by its omnipresent, efficacious call.

With their colourful plumage
and ability to perform daring
feats of aerobatics, hou faeries
mimic the hummingbirds
from our world. These small
faeries produce low humming
sounds which seem to be a
form of echolocation. Their
feeding habits differ from the
hummingbird's, however, as they
secrete a digestive enzyme that
causes their desired food to dissolve
into a potable liquid.

Underneath its branches, hopes, dreams, and downfalls will be revealed as the Tree of All softly sings prophecy into your ear. The Tree provides shelter, safety, and knowledge to all who seek it. However, those with malice in their hearts will feel the pain and anguish they have inflicted, or will inflict, on other living beings, driving them to madness and despair. The Tree will eventually claim their soul and leave them to die at its roots. As their bodies decay, they become nourishment to this ancient and all-powerful being. Enter freely if your soul is pure, and the Tree may murmur wondrous things in your ear.

The smaller bird faeries like to
stay safe and travel in flocks.
In summer, just before dusk,
these whimsical faeries can
be seen dancing in the sky,
performing something best
described as ballet. They are
an inquisitive bunch and like
to tap on windows to draw
attention, only to quickly fly
away when you look up.

In wintertime when food is scarce, the bird faeries will raid bird feeders. They love fancy teacups filled with peanut butter and enjoy taking long, relaxing soaks in bird baths in summer. It can be difficult to distinguish these faeries from real birds, but if you look closely you will see that they have feet instead of claws. Some don't even have fully developed wings, but rather tiny arms with feathers growing out of them.

Bird faeries of a more
advanced age prefer to
take the form of the
solitary, nocturnal
owl. While the smaller
bird faeries love to
adorn themselves
with vivid plumage,
these creatures prefer
earthy, natural
colours that enable
them to stay hidden
and observe the world.

101

These old and wise spirits glide
soundlessly through the darkness.
They act as messengers and
sometimes carry the very young
or small deep into the Faultlines.
It is believed their hooting, which
is reminiscent of an owl but with
a distinctly higher pitch, brings
tidings of ill fortune. However,
I've found no evidence to confirm
this to be true.

My belief is that these faeries'
haunting, glowing gaze drives
onlookers to despair as it pierces
their souls, revealing all that
is hidden and forgotten in the
darkness.

The harpy is a fierce
and dangerous
creature that's
able to lift a grown
man into the air
in their strong
talons. They enjoy playing
a cruel game, carrying
their prey high into the
air only to suddenly drop
them, letting them fall
to the ground or catching
them just in time.
A dark shadow passing
overhead might be a
harpy circling around
and looking for prey.

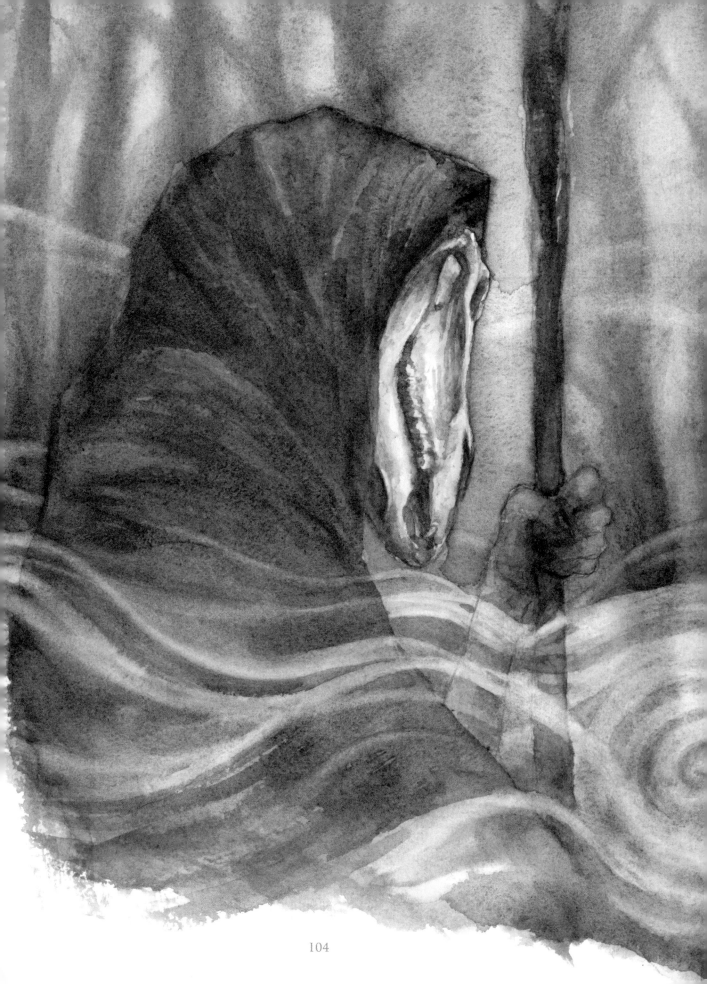

of the

WITCH

During my stays in remote parts of the Faultlines, I came across some creatures that changed my perception of faeries entirely. One may call them witches, although I don't believe this to be an accurate name for them as they have little to do with the beings of lore and myth. Like all faeries, they are magical creatures. What they do have in common with the witches from classic fairy tales is that most can shapeshift, cast spells, and brew potions. And yes, their facial features include hooked noses, mouths filled with gnarly, pointed teeth, and piercing eyes.

The similarities end there. As the witches and hags of the Faultlines are so diverse in their magic and appearance, it would do them a disservice to describe them as mere old women using magic. These faeries choose their form based on necessity: they can take the shape of beautiful young women or the form of objects, like standing stones. Some may stay in their preferred form for too long, rendering them unable to shed it and return to their former appearance. These faeries are known to draw strength and knowledge from their surroundings, tapping into trees – or even stones – to gain their ancient wisdom. They are of great importance and purpose, and neither wholly malevolent nor benevolent. Rather, they are the keepers of balance. They can bring nightmares or beautiful dreams, sickness or good health. They influence the elements, give true or false counsel, and may either lead travellers the way or astray. In short, they do what they feel must be done to maintain balance in the Faultlines.

Familiars are spirits in the guise of creatures such as birds, snakes, rodents, toads, or cats. These creatures aid witches with their magic and offer them protection. A familiar's bond is the source of the witch's power.

The Raven Mage wears a black
coat made of raven feathers.
Dark as the night sky, it
enables her to soundlessly
soar through the air and
to be seen by no one.

The Mage brings darkness in her wake, and some would
even say seeing her is an omen of death. Even so, her
arrival marks the end of pain and sorrow. She is kin to
the Morrigan, the triple goddess of death and destiny.

The black feathers of the
raven witch contain some of the
darkest magic. Using one of these
feathers to put a curse upon
someone else will mark
your soul forever. This
mark is like a beacon to
the raven witch, always
keeping an eye on you
until the day she
decides it is time to
claim your soul.

A raven witch prefers the form
of a raven. As she ages, she slowly
loses her ability and desire to
transform back to her original
humanoid form. Once this
form is lost to her forever,
she becomes unable to
communicate the way
she used to and can
no longer share her
vast wisdom.

The nykr, or nicker, are water spirits I encountered while I was hiking across some wetlands. I was so enthralled by the beautiful landscape that I didn't watch where I was going until my foot got stuck in a bog.

I then felt their hands
wrapping around my ankle,
trying to drag me down.
I only managed to free
myself by offering them
some of the tiny white
butterflies I had caught
earlier, which are
apparently something
of a delicacy to these
spirits.

Their sickly brown and
green skin is thick and
leathery like that of
a peat body that has lain
submerged under the dark
surface for centuries.

111

The murky waters of the Faultlines are home to the nykr. The dirty, dark water provides them with the perfect cover to lie waiting in ambush. They have no dietary restrictions – whatever finds its way into their clutches nourishes them – but it is said they prefer the sweet and tender meat of human children. They can stay underwater for a very long time, rarely rising to the surface to breathe. When they do, only their glowing white eyes are visible, as their otherwise dark features hide them from sight. Their thin, dark, and long hair allows them to cover the water's surface, creating the illusion of solid ground. Once a child steps on this treacherous surface, they will find themselves ensnared in the dark tangle of the nykr's hair, choke, and drown. I suspect that these creatures are one and the same as Jenny Greenteeth, Peg Powler, and the Shellycoat, or at the least of close relation. More research and observation on the nature and habitat of the nykr is certainly needed.

One day, I stumbled upon a solitary standing stone
on the moors. I detected the faint, delicate facial
features of a woman as well as markings carved into
the surface of the stone. The symbols, lines, and
swirls tracing her cold skin seemed to move slightly.
Although I hardly noticed it at first, it dawned
on me that this standing stone was alive and even
seemed to breathe. I've been told her powers are
kept under control by a potent magic that keeps her
trapped in her prison. Once the light of the full
moon touches her skin, she can break free from her
confinement long enough to lure travellers with her
mesmerizing and hard-hearted gaze, imploring them
to lay a hand on her ice-cold skin. Upon doing so, they
will find their doom in the water beneath her feet
and become a swirl etched on her body.

Upon closer observation and research I have discovered that there are many types of standing stones, some quite dangerous and many quite harmless. There is one group of stones so powerful and dangerous it is best avoided. Known as the Silent Sisters, these sister witch stones are anything but silent. You can hear their voices in the air whispering enchantments, frantically searching for ways to break free from their stone prisons. The Sisters are known to use magic to force travellers to fall asleep on the soft grasses near their stony feet. Whilst the traveller sleeps, their essence is drained away, leaving them empty. When morning breaks and the traveller awakes, all sense of being will be lost to them, and they will no longer know where, who, or even what they are. Each soul the Silent Sisters collect brings them one step closer to freedom.

120

A willow witch, or sealh, is the
spirit of a witch inhabiting a
willow tree. It's not always
easy to spot a tree in which
a sealh has hidden her soul,
but sometimes her face can be
seen in its gnarly bark. Some
sealh are malevolent and will
stalk travellers passing by
their willows. Most, however,
are benevolent and enjoy a good
conversation. With their roots
in the spirit world, they know
much. If you seek answers,
it is always worth asking a
willow witch.

The Bone Collector
is as old as time and
collects the bones of
the dead. She keeps
them carefully tucked
inside her coat of human
hair. She grinds them
into dust and then blows it
into the eyes of those whose
time is up. She decides the
fate of the living and any
unfortunate soul whose bones
she means to collect.

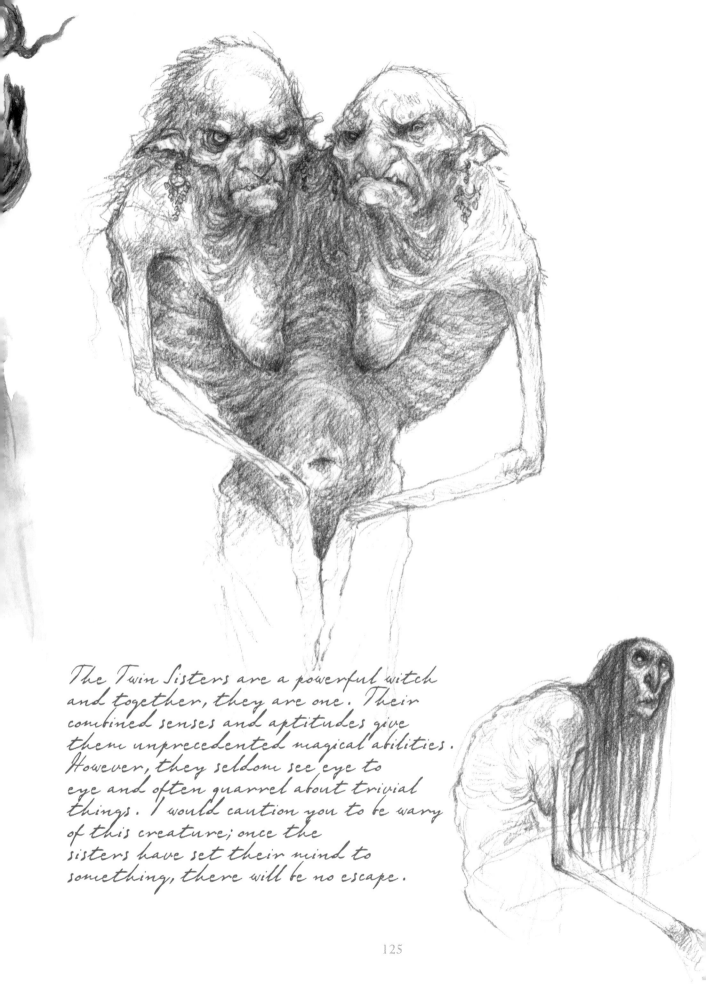

The Twin Sisters are a powerful witch and together, they are one. Their combined senses and aptitudes give them unprecedented magical abilities. However, they seldom see eye to eye and often quarrel about trivial things. I would caution you to be wary of this creature; once the sisters have set their mind to something, there will be no escape.

Each woods witch is carefully
chosen by a tree to perform
the ritual of the "Choosing,"
which is one of the most
important and most difficult
known feats of magic. Performed
during the last full moon of the
year, this ritual determines the
past, present, and future of both
tree and witch and merges their
souls together as one. Over time, the
witch's body will grow into the tree and
become a living part of it, tapping deeper
and deeper into the soul of her host
and gradually absorbing its knowledge.
With their roots digging deep into
the earth where the purest magic
can be found, the woods witches stay
connected to each other by means of
the elaborate root systems of the
trees they inhabit. Whatever
one of the woods witches knows,
the others know as well.

The rjúkjare is a witch whose hair is so long and dark it continually billows and undulates like smoke in the wind. She often disappears as quickly and silently as she emerges. Getting caught in the dark tangle of her hair means certain death. The rjúkjare appears to float rather than walk, and glides through the air without making a single sound!

It's not uncommon to find troll witches.
They are particularly brutal creatures
that possess a twisted and ancient magic.
They control the lower creatures that
live in the dirt and mud, and it is these
centipedes, tadpoles, and the occasional newt
that do their bidding.

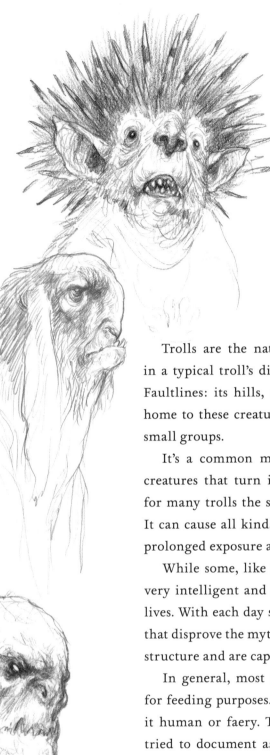

of the

TROLL

Trolls are the natural enemies of most faeries, the main ingredient in a typical troll's diet. They can be found dwelling in every part of the Faultlines: its hills, mountains, streams, marshes, and even trees are all home to these creatures. While some are solitary creatures, others live in small groups.

It's a common misconception that all trolls are brutal, flesh-eating creatures that turn into stone when exposed to sunlight. It is true that for many trolls the sun, or rather ultraviolet light, is extremely harmful. It can cause all kinds of skin problems and for some the consequences of prolonged exposure are even worse than a nasty rash or odd growth.

While some, like the *bëule* troll, are incredibly dim-witted, others are very intelligent and have learned to use tools to help them in their daily lives. With each day spent in the Faultlines I discover new species of trolls that disprove the myth of the blundering beast. Many have a complex social structure and are capable of creating beauty.

In general, most trolls don't seek out any other creatures unless it is for feeding purposes. They prefer to live far away from any habitation, be it human or faery. There is significant diversity in the species, and I've tried to document as many as I could to give an accurate overview. For instance, there are the nocturnal hedgetrolls that are distant cousins to our hedgehogs, who like to rummage through the leaves and dirt. Compared to other troll species they are rather small, as they are no bigger than a four-year-old child. And then there are the *sümpf* trolls. These nasty, slime-covered creatures hide underneath roots as they wait for fresh meat to come along (which they prefer to eat raw).

When rute trolls get to a certain age,
they start growing branches from their
bodies. Their hardened skin resembles the
bark of a tree. Young rute trolls are docile,
but as they age they become dangerous.
Older rute trolls might be slower, but
their limbs are larger and stronger,
allowing them to lash out, snap their
branches on your body, and knock you
to the ground in the blink of an eye.

132

The sümpf troll lurks between
the roots of trees. It is difficult
to spot amongst the vegetation
as its body closely resembles the
moss-covered roots where it tends
to hide, waiting to grab its victims
with its long arms and fingers.
When meat is scarce, it will
survive on insects or worms, using
its sticky, long tongue to quickly
snap them up. Watch out when
you hear a loud croaking call like
that of a bullfrog, for a sümpf
troll may be lurking nearby.

The schøppetroll is
a bashful, skittish
creature that curls
up in a ball rather like
a pangolin. It can stay
curled up, mimicking a rock,
for a long time.

Fløte trolls can imitate every bird whistle in the Faultlines and produce the most beautiful songs to lure them in. Once close, the fløte, using its club, will knock a bird out of the air and eat it whole.

Kind-hearted stinkhörn trolls are incredibly rare and hardly ever seen. To hide from other more brutal trolls, these slow-moving creatures have developed a symbiotic relationship with the various flora growing on their bodies. Plants and fungi have become part of their anatomy and get nutrients from the troll's body. In return, they help protect it against possible threats. When frightened, the stinkhörn troll releases spores into the air, producing a horrible smell that lingers for days and keeps predators at bay.

The ears of the bëule troll never
stop growing, and as they age these
long ears become a sign of fertility
and strength. To avoid tripping
over them or entangling them
in undergrowth or thicket,
these trolls will wrap their
ears around their bodies. This
is particularly pleasant in
wintertime as it helps keep
them warm.

The bëule troll has
a tiny brain in its
large skull. The bigger
the bony bump on its
head, the bigger the
advantage a troll has
during a fight. This
bump may also be used
for breaking rocks when
foraging.

141

A mief is as blind as a bat. These trolls have developed a highly sensitive sense of smell to compensate for their blindness. Their noses are flexible because they have no cartilage; instead, they have a big muscle which can move independently, much like the trunk of an elephant, although the mief troll is unable to grasp things with it. Miefs use their horns to dig up precious fungi from the dirt. They have tiny hairs all over their bodies to help them detect even the slightest changes in the air. Fortunately for miefs, they smell so terrible that they don't have to fear many predators.

There is some truth to the fairy tales about trolls turning into stone at sunrise. However, this doesn't affect all troll species. There are some that are more vulnerable to ultraviolet light. The skin of these trolls will harden and start to resemble stone as soon as it's exposed to the light. This will not kill the troll. Instead, over time, the troll will become trapped in a hard, stone-like shell, remaining aware of its surroundings but unable to move or speak. Suffering a fate worse than death, these stone trolls will bleed if you prick them and if you listen very carefully you can hear their heartbeat.

of the

GNOME, HOBGOBLIN, & BROWNIE

The Faultlines is teeming with subspecies of faeries known as gnomes, hobgoblins, and brownies. These unusual – and very often mischievous – chaps are all part of a particular branch of the faery family. All three vary in stature: most are very small and no bigger than a mouse, whereas others can be as large as a domestic cat or even a two-year-old child. I've been told that some are also able to change size depending on necessity.

Their appearances all have much in common; therefore, it is sometimes difficult to differentiate the various species. Indeed, they all look like small, extremely hairy men with prominent, gnarly, and wrinkly facial features. Some hobgoblins and brownies look slightly like rodents; this makes it easy for them to blend in with the mice scurrying about the house. Since I have not encountered any female hobgoblins or brownies I suspect they are all male. Female gnomes look very much like their male equivalents but lack their facial hair, although their noses are as prominent.

Gnomes are more peaceful creatures than either hobgoblins or brownies. They don't live in human dwellings but instead prefer to live in comfortable holes underground or in trees. Whereas brownies and hobgoblins are often naked, wearing nothing apart from something resembling a pair of trousers, gnomes wear clothes to protect themselves from the elements.

They use whatever nature provides, such as cobwebs and deer fur, to create their clothing. Their brightly coloured, pointy hat is their most distinctive feature and sets them apart from hobgoblins and brownies. The colour of the hat, obtained by dying the material using berries and all kinds of plants, signifies a gnome's status in life, making it easy to communicate over long distance if one is, for instance, unattached or looking for a companion, or warning others to stay well away.

Unlike brownies and hobgoblins, gnomes don't expect payment for their services. Just like the former, they do very much enjoy a little mischief from time to time and love to play tricks on travellers, popping up out of nowhere only to quickly vanish, leaving a puzzled traveller behind.

All three species are known to be very obliging, helping with simple chores in and around the house. Hobgoblins choose a person – or sometimes family – with whom they will live for the rest of their lives. However, for all their good intentions, hobgoblins do not always help. Sometimes they like to play tricks, mess things up, or hide valuable items.

Brownies, like hobgoblins, can often be found in human residences but don't stay with just one person or family, instead choosing to frequently visit different households on the same street or within a village. It is important to note they expect payment for their help; this can be anything from buttons to coins and other shiny objects.

Gnomes have a very kind and giving nature and tending to things and other beings is what they love to do. They take care of the small things and creatures of the Faultlines, like insects, moss, and orphaned animals.

Gnomes use their brightly
coloured, pointy hats to keep
their valuables safely tucked
away. These hats are commonly
made of fur, wool, or mushrooms,
and are often dyed with berries.

149

If you leave any valuable items lying around the house, hobgoblins and brownies will take them, considering it payment for their help. A gnome might take something too, but only to shine it up and leave it in a safer place for you, though you may never find out, or find your valuables again.

You might be in for a nasty surprise if you anger a hobgoblin or brownie. They are known to turn milk sour, make holes in your favourite socks, and leave stones in your shoes as punishment for treating them poorly.

of the

PIZKIE

It is in the nature of faeries to play tricks on humans. Their mischievous character can be a bother, and in some cases even very dangerous. While brownies and hobgoblins are among the most common, there are a lot of faeries that belong to the pizkie species of faery. These creatures come in all shapes and sizes, and their tricks are ordinarily quite harmless. However, some do possess properties and traits that pose a threat to the well-being of humans and other faeries. For instance, there are pizkies whose touch can cause severe blisters on the skin and there are those who release a toxin that can leave a potential predator disoriented for days. Though mostly harmless, for humans these pizkie tricks can cause some serious, sometimes unintended, side effects.

Pizkies predominantly choose to live far away from any human activity. However there are those who prefer to reside in our homes and have adapted to a life alongside humans. I myself have a pizkie named Nunoo living in my studio. This little creature, about the size of a rat, has a blue and green coloured body that is covered in soft spike-like protrusions. I first discovered this little fellow rummaging around in a bin. It was apparently looking for something, continuously shaking his little head and muttering *"nunoo-nunoo!"* which then prompted his name. Whenever he found something to his liking, he would put it in his little pouch and continue to look for more.

Nunoo has become a welcome sight in my studio and I often leave small items for him to add to his collection. There are, however, creatures lurking in the house I'm not as fond of. One of them enjoys playing with my house keys, and one even relishes in the destruction of my socks. Keeping house pizkies happy and occupied prevents them from playing tricks on you.

Nuks are playful little pikzies
that wiggle their ears when they
are happy and are known to be
very fond of strawberry jam and
chocolate sprinkles. They are
generally very inquisitive in
nature, but also a little
shy and easily spooked.
Because of their highly
developed and acute sense
of hearing, they can hear
each and every little sound.

Bookwurms devour books, rare prints,
magazines, and even precious pieces of art.
These creatures can absorb ink from paper
into their bloodstream, which then creates
distinctive markings on their fur. These
markings are unique to the males of the
species, and the spectacle-like pattern
around their eyes is considered highly
attractive to the females.

155

Old, dirty socks are this vivid winged faery's preferred snack. This creature is responsible for leaving holes in your socks due to his habit of tasting them before deciding which one to eat. Sometimes, when socks are scarce, underwear will do.

I found a rykögn under my bed not too long ago. These little faeries are often covered in long, grey-coloured hair that they use to collect dust, which they then roll up in large balls and carry around with them in their long arms. The rykögn have huge, black eyes that are perfectly adapted to life in the dark, hard-to-reach places underneath sofas or beds that hardly ever see a vacuum cleaner.

The tiny hairs that cover
the body of this faery attach
themselves to a person or
predator's skin upon touch.
At first, this rather tingly
feeling is a pleasant one, making
the affected part of the body
feel warm and fuzzy. But if
these areas are left untreated,
blisters will start to form, giving
the phrase "kissed by faeries."
a wholly different meaning.

Tufts are often mistaken for
their cousins, the straysods.
Both look like small patches of
grass or weeds and are difficult
to distinguish from normal
vegetation. Unlike their
malevolent cousins, tufts don't
bite the ankles of passersby
but rather release a toxin in
the air that induces a natural
high when inhaled.

The titillatus, or tickler, has long fingers ideal for tickling and possesses a self-defence mechanism like that of certain insects. They are covered in tiny, bristly hairs that detach themselves when touched. These hairs then secrete a venom that is absorbed by the body and will irritate the skin around the affected area, leaving an unfortunate person or predator itchy for days.

A likyll pizkie is fond of keys. Their gnawing on the metal is the reason why sometimes keys no longer fit. I suspect they are responsible for always hiding the keys in places you never think to look.

This little, fat faery loves to steal buttons from garments. It seems he's very particular about the material the button is made of, and I've seen him vigorously check every single button before deciding which one to eat.

Toothfaeries have a very keen sense of smell. Due to their double set of nostrils that scour the air for the smell of rot, they can detect the scent of tooth decay from miles away. Travelling in packs, each of the faeries is appointed a specific task in the teeth gathering process. A couple will stand guard as a small group keeps the mouth open, allowing the others to then climb inside and pick away at the rotten tooth. Their bodies are covered in tooth-like armoured scales that protect them from injury should they ever get trapped inside a mouth! They communicate with clicking sounds that resemble the chattering or gnashing of teeth.

The fearsome-looking garga hunts by using a form of echolocation and finds her way by shrieking. The way her wails bounce back from an object tells this creature if her prey is still alive or already dead. She prefers to eat the latter.

A banshee's wail is believed to
be a bad omen that heralds
imminent death.

This horned dragon
has an excellent
sense of smell and
filters the air
through his many
nasal cavities, sniffing
out the subtle hints
of different scents.
It is said the smell
of fear appeals to him
the most.

166

of the

DRAGON

The dragons of the Faultlines are rich in both numbers and diversity. There are small, feathered species no bigger than sparrows that live in packs, and massive behemoths that dwell in the volcanic mountains where they lie dormant. Many earthquakes and volcanic eruptions can be attributed to these creatures. I've not witnessed *The Waking** myself but have heard tales from ancient times of the destruction wrought upon the Faultlines when one of these creatures awoke from slumber.

There are dragons everywhere, from the deserts to the seas, all perfectly adapted to their respective territories. Some can fly high up in the air with feathered wings that look like they are made of gold and precious stones. Others live in trees and rarely touch the forest floors except on rare occasions such as mating, for example. Polychromatic specimens are as prevalent as those that have completely adjusted to a life hidden from sight, their bodies covered in the same vegetation that surrounds them. There are even dragons that adapt their appearance entirely according to their surroundings much like chameleons do.

While dragons aren't capable of speech, they do have a language best described as a form of communication that utilizes clicks, grunts, and even high-pitched avian sounds to communicate across vast distances. These magnificent creatures have various means of defending themselves, such as fire, venom, sharp teeth, piercing claws, or in some cases even a mighty tail, or spikes all over their bodies.

---

* *The most ancient and powerful of dragons are sleeping in the mountains and volcanoes of the Faultlines. It is said when one or more of these ancient ones awakens, balance will be restored at great cost. A true* Waking *hasn't happened in a long time but I've felt the earth rumble underneath my feet. The balance is respected and kept by all faeries – it is us humans who threaten it.*

This dragon, affectionately known as the whubwhub, is one of the smallest in the Faultlines and similar in size to a Pekinese dog. Named after the sound it produces when it bobs its head up and down and inflates its throat sac, a whubwhub can change colour depending on its mood. A fierce creature that puffs up its feathers to make itself appear larger when threatened, the whubwhub also has venom glands that produce a highly flammable and irritating poison. Its mouth is filled with lamellae just like the ones common ducks have.

Some dragons use the bump on their head for echolocation. They can produce many different sounds ranging from high-pitched squealing noises to deep, low rumbling ones.

Listening carefully to the echoes of the sound waves, these dragons can locate their prey even in dark or misty environments where eyesight is useless.

Eik dragons dwell in the
oldest parts of the forest
and were the first dragons
to inhabit the Faultlines.
Younger eik dragons move
with the rhythm of the
forest's trees, following
the sway of the branches
when they hop from tree
to tree. They get their
nourishment from feeding
off the dead, rotten wood.
The older eik dragons
slowly become rooted.
No longer able to move
along the tree branches, they
become one with the forest.
The gentle vibration of their slow
breathing can be felt when you
place your hand on their bark.

Eldrir dragons are often mistaken for the mythical phoenix because of their vibrant gold plumage that makes them appear to be on fire. These dragons love to fly as close to the sun as possible in order to recharge their energy. Their spectacular air dances are truly a sight to behold and are often confused with solar flares.

When fully charged, they can use the power stored inside them to breathe fire so hot it will melt any material. These dragons have been hunted close to extinction because of their brilliant feathers.

The imposing horns of the horing dragons
never stop growing. Throughout the life
of the horing new horn-like protrusions
sprout from the skull and even the rest of
the body. The horns look heavy but are,
for the most part, hollow.
As they grow they furl
into intricate curls and
shapes. These more
brittle parts will break
during an altercation
between two horing dragons.
This doesn't seem to affect the
horing much and the horn will
continue to grow. These snapped
off parts of the horing horn
look like dead tree branches.
Sometimes you can find lots of
these on the forest floor, a clear
sign there has been a fight.

The lore dragon, more commonly referred to as the flower dragon or petal dragon, is one of the smallest species I have encountered in the Faultlines. The largest specimens of this species are female and about the size of a human hand; the males are slightly smaller but are adorned with more vibrantly coloured petals. These chromatic creatures can be found hunting insect faeries in the fields and meadows of the Faultlines. They seem to have a very complex social structure and their graceful flight is a mesmerizing spectacle at the dusky hours of the day. More is to be discovered about this enthralling creature.

of the

MERMAID

The oceans, lakes, rivers, streams, and even the marshes and bogs of the Faultlines are populated by aquatic faeries. While some of them are able to flourish in the deep as well as on land, many of these water-dwelling creatures are ill-adapted to life outside of their marine environment and seldom venture onto dry land.

In popular folklore, these half-fish, half-humanoid faeries are called mermaids or mermen.* According to myth, these creatures are incredibly stunning to behold and will drag unfortunate sailors to their untimely deaths in the fathoms below. However, this name doesn't cover the entire species of aquatic faeries. Strictly speaking, creatures such as sylkies, kelpies, and the nykr aren't mermaids, even though all of them spend most of their lives in the water.

Both kelpies and sylkies can shapeshift into beautiful, young creatures that closely resemble humans. Not all aquatic beings are able to do this. The faeries living deep in the oceans are unable to surface as their anatomy is so adapted to living under high pressure that they would die upon emerging from the water, as a result of their inability to withstand the dramatic change of pressure and to breathe air.

The diet of a mermaid is restricted to whatever they can forage on the ocean floor and what is brought down to them by the many storms at sea. These beings look nothing like the mermaids of lore and can be as dangerous as the environment they live in. Life underwater is perilous, so mermaids have developed a variety of skills and methods to survive.

---

* *The terms* mermaid *and* merman *are human constructs placed on these faeries out of confusion or lack of knowledge. As gender is not part of faery life, I will simply use the term* mermaids *when talking about aquatic faeries. The confusion may stem from the fact that, like most faeries, mermaids are able to change sex if the need calls for it. As these aquatic faeries live in some of the most hostile environments of the Faultlines this ability is a matter of survival.*

Male aquatic faeries are a less common
sight. One possible reason for this
might be the fact they display
highly territorial behaviour. The
often dangerous and deadly fights
that ensue between them tend to
diminish their numbers significantly.
The females, however, have more subtle
ways of fighting for their territory.

The gegnsøtt live in the deepest, coldest, and darkest parts of the oceans. This nearly translucent and almost ghostlike faery is difficult to spot in the water. As eyesight isn't of much use in these dark places, this mermaid has appendages on its face that allow the faery to detect potential prey, stalk it without being noticed, and quickly snap it up.

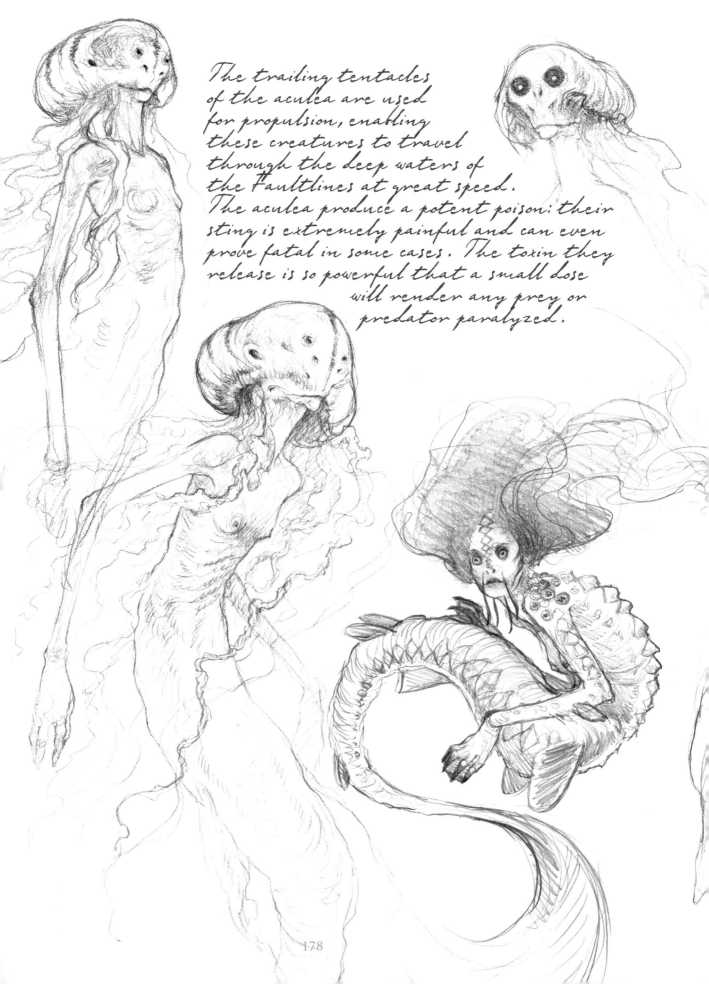

The trailing tentacles
of the aculea are used
for propulsion, enabling
these creatures to travel
through the deep waters of
the Faultlines at great speed.
The aculea produce a potent poison: their
sting is extremely painful and can even
prove fatal in some cases. The toxin they
release is so powerful that a small dose
will render any prey or
predator paralyzed.

The sylkies are maidens of the deep that can transform into human or seal form. These curious creatures are interested in the world of man and enjoy basking in the sun for hours. The ocean is their home, and even though they can spend years ashore they will always long for the sea. A sylky living on dry land has genuine sorrow in her eyes. This sadness will continue to grow and finally kill her unless she returns to her home under the sea. Once there, the sylky will continue to visit and watch over the loved ones she left behind.

179

The vuokkal or reef-dwelling mermaid comes in all shapes, sizes, and colours, but every member of the species has a body that is covered in tentacles that can retract or expand to catch prey. These appendages contain venomous stinging cells used to ward off predators or subdue prey. Their mouth is filled with small, razor-sharp teeth and the feathery tentacles encircling them are used to smell their surroundings. They are capable of finding prey even when it's hidden under the sand.

The highly intelligent
pulpo mermaid is a true
master of camouflage.
Much like their namesake,
the octopus, they have
the ability to change their
colour in an instant,
using this colour- and
even pattern-changing
ability when hunting,
communicating,
or to simply avoid
predators.

Skulp mermaids live in the shallow tide pools
of the rocky shores of the Faultlines. Life
in these pools is difficult and only the most
resilient of mermaids are able to withstand
the frequent flood and drain of the tides.
The danger of being swept to open sea or left
in the scorching heat when the pools dry
up is one these hardy creatures face daily.

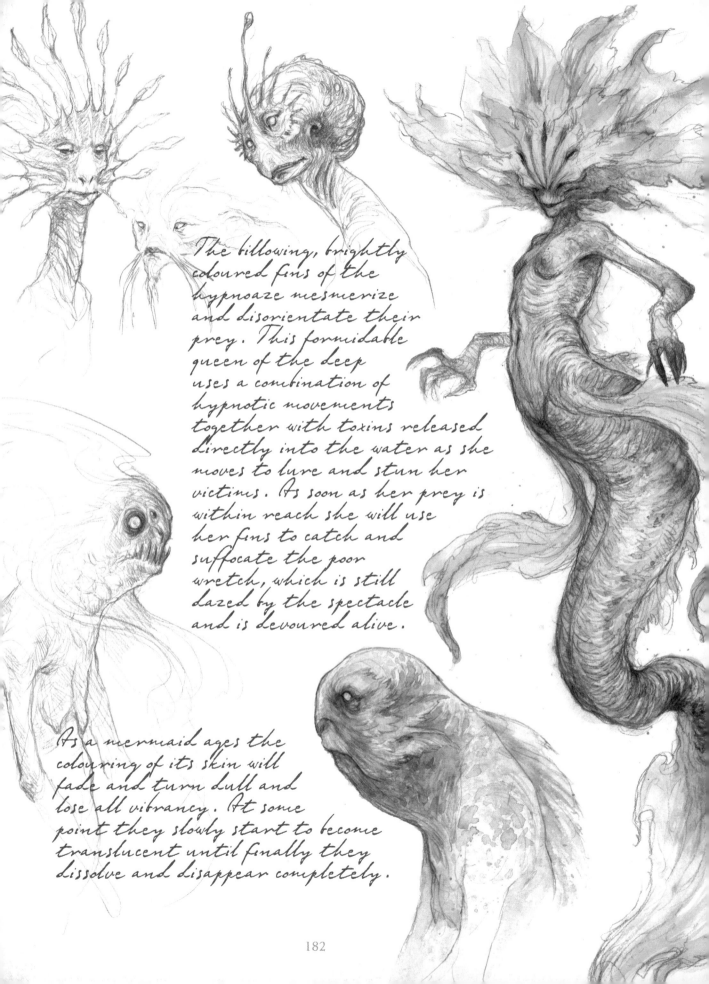

The billowing, brightly coloured fins of the hypnoaze mesmerize and disorientate their prey. This formidable queen of the deep uses a combination of hypnotic movements together with toxins released directly into the water as she moves to lure and stun her victims. As soon as her prey is within reach she will use her fins to catch and suffocate the poor wretch, which is still dazed by the spectacle and is devoured alive.

As a mermaid ages the colouring of its skin will fade and turn dull and lose all vibrancy. At some point they slowly start to become translucent until finally they dissolve and disappear completely.

Faeries of the Faultlines: Edited, Expanded Edition

Published by Eye of Newt Books Inc.
www.eyeofnewtpress.com
Eye of Newt Books Inc.
56 Edith Drive, Toronto, Ontario, M4R 1C3

First printed 2018 by Iris Compiet,
Second edition, *Faeries of the Faultlines: Edited, Expanded Edition*,
printed 2021 by Eye of Newt Books
Second edition, second printing 2023 by Eye of Newt Books

Iris Compiet
www.iriscompiet.art
www.faeriesofthefaultlines.com

ISBN 978-1-7770817-2-0

Printed in China

A thank you to everyone who made the first edition possible! This new edition would not have been possible if not for your support of the first. Thank you to Neil, Danny, and Stephanie at Eye of Newt Books for believing in the faeries and in me. Bart for his love, patience, and support. A thank you to Brian Froud and Alan Lee for not only inspiring me all those years ago to pursue a dream of becoming an artist but also for their words and kindness towards my faeries. Thank you as well to John Howe, Guillermo del Toro, and Tony DiTerlizzi for their words and continued inspiration. And finally, a thank you to the faeries, for allowing me to enter the Faultlines and share the path with the world.